STORIES NEVER TOLD

VOLUME 1

STORIES NEVER TOLD

VOLUME 1

ROSE WILLS

DAVID WOMACK WILLS
(POSTHUMOUSLY)

authorHOUSE®

AuthorHouse™
1663 Liberty Drive
Bloomington, IN 47403
www.authorhouse.com
Phone: 1-800-839-8640

Published by AuthorHouse   06/05/2012

ISBN: 978-1-4772-0994-3 (sc)
ISBN: 978-1-4772-0993-6 (e)

Library of Congress Control Number: 2012909191

Any people depicted in stock imagery provided by Thinkstock are models,
and such images are being used for illustrative purposes only.
Certain stock imagery © Thinkstock.

This book is printed on acid-free paper.

CONTENTS

Preface		vii
Chapter 1	Poem (Patricia C. Wills)	1
Chapter 2	The Legend of the Woman Without a Heart	2
Chapter 3	The King of the Birds	3
Chapter 4	A Remedy Against Pain	4
Chapter 5	The Wizard Called John	5
Chapter 6	Why Are Crows Black	6
Chapter 7	Peter and the Cow	7
Chapter 8	A Proof of Love	9
Chapter 9	Eyes Up (Patricia C. Wills)	10
Chapter 10	Falling From the Donkey	11
Chapter 11	The Big Elephant	12
Chapter 12	Why People Die	13
Chapter 13	The Ungrateful Lion	14
Chapter 14	The Lying Irishman	15
Chapter 15	The Monkey and the Turtle	16
Chapter 16	Bob and the Robin	18
Chapter 17	Yen and Yang	19
Chapter 18	Heaven and Hell	20
Chapter 19	The Fox and the Duck	21
Chapter 20	The Mouse and the Cat	22
Chapter 21	The History of Miami Beach	23
Chapter 22	The River and the Horse	25
Chapter 23	The Eagle and the Wren	26
Chapter 24	The Camel and the Ant	27
Chapter 25	The Vane Giraffe	28
Chapter 26	The Fox and the Rooster	29
Chapter 27	The Genies of the Fireplace	30
Chapter 28	The Carpenter and the Trunk	31
Chapter 29	The Donkey and the Tiger	32
Chapter 30	Elizabeth's Questions	34
Chapter 31	The Three Daughters	35
Chapter 32	The Bold Man	37
Chapter 33	Kim's Rabbit	38
Chapter 34	The Basil's Girl	40
Chapter 35	The Magic Ring	42

Chapter 36	The Story of the Elephant Trunk	43
Chapter 37	The Pigeon and the Ant	44
Chapter 38	The Flower and the Snail	45
Chapter 39	The Vain Crow	46
Chapter 40	The Wolf and the Crane	47
Chapter 41	Que Up—No Showing (David Womack Wills)	48
Chapter 42	Suspicion (David Womack Wills)	49
Chapter 43	Tranquil (David Womack Wills)	50
Chapter 44	Up The Clock, Doc (David Womack Wills)	51
Chapter 45	A Cat Named Fifi	53
Chapter 46	Your 55 1/2 Year Birthday (David Womack Wills)	54
Chapter 47	The Sly Turtle	55
Chapter 48	The Legend of the Corals	56
Chapter 49	The Wizard's Daughter	57
Chapter 50	Why The Sun is in the Sky	58
Chapter 51	Peanut	59
Chapter 52	The Sun in Love	60
Chapter 53	An Endless Story	61
Chapter 54	Why We Have Deserts	62
Chapter 55	The Baby Stolen by the Fairies	63
Chapter 56	The Man Fish	64
Chapter 57	The Magic Roast	65
Chapter 58	The Legend of the Poison Ivy	66
Chapter 59	Why the Chicken Scratches the Earth	67
Chapter 60	The Girl of the Melon	68
Chapter 61	Valentine Day—2007 (David Womack Wills)	69
Chapter 62	Christmas in the Air Force (David Womack Wills)	70
Chapter 63	Soixante (David Womack Wills)	71
Chapter 64	Valentine Day 2001 36 Years (David Womack Wills)	72
Chapter 65	37 Years Anniversary (David Womack Wills)	74
Chapter 66	39 Years Wow! (David Womack Wills)	76
Chapter 67	Valentine 2003 and All Those Years (David Womack Wills)	77
Chapter 68	Merry Christmas 2004 (David Womack Wills)	79
Chapter 69	Mother's Day—2005 (David Womack Wills)	80
Chapter 70	Another Birthday (David Womack Wills)	81

PREFACE

At 6 years old, "Mommy, I love you"
At 10 years old, "Mom, whatever"
At 16 years old, "My mom is so annoying"
At 18 years old, "I wanna leave this house."
At 25 years old, "Mom, you were right."
At 30 years old, "I wanna go to Mom's house."
At 50 years old, "I don't wanna lose my Mom."
At 70 years old, "I would give up Everything for my Mom to be here with me"

CHAPTER 1

POEM
BY
PATRICIA C. WILLS

Wind in my face, mane in my hands
Power and grace, beauty and fire
Ears set forward, never look back.
Earth rushing quickly
Beneath, we are racing!
Hear steady hoof beats,
Like musical notes, we dance
On the staff of the bass clef.
And then I sit back,
Tentative wars flicker
It's time to slow down,
Time to turn around . . .
We'll dance again some other day,
We'll soar again to another place,

I know you'll keep me safe . . . .

CHAPTER 2

THE LEGEND OF THE WOMAN WITHOUT A HEART

Many years ago, a very rich woman lived in a castle. She owned many lands. Her name was Lady Mary. She was known for being selfish, greedy and no feelings. The farmers that worked her land were paid very little money, and they worked more than 12 hours a day. During the summer, a drought came along, and the villagers were risking starving to death. Only Lady Mary could provide enough food and more to everyone. But she was worried only about herself, and if she had enough food for her beautiful white horse, her only love. She used to ride to inspect the lands that she owned.

One day during one of her riding, she met a man. The man said, "Have pity on me, I am old and tired, please give me something to eat, please, I beg you."

The man had just seen Lady Mary give food and sweets to her horse.

The woman did not answer and kept on riding.

The man again, "please give me something to eat, in the name of God."

The lady turned around and threw him a stone, "If you are really hungry, then eat this stone."

And the man, "May you change in stone, may this stone take the place of your heart."

The man was a wizard; he had been called by the farmers that worked for Lady Mary. The woman became a rock, and so did her horse, the castle and all her land. The farmers never told anyone.

CHAPTER 3

THE KING OF THE BIRDS

Once upon a time the birds decided to proclaim a king. They got together and decided that the king should be the wisest of them all, the Owl.

The raven came late to the reunion, and was quite angry, "Why are you choosing that old Owl as a king? The one that will protect us the most has to be smart; remember the story of the heron and the crab?"

The other birds did not remember it so the crow starts narrating it.

"Long time ago there was an old heron that could not catch fishes. So he decided to play smart; he went to the middle of the lake and started crying. The fishes asked him what was wrong, and he said that humans were planning to dry out the lake, so all the fish will die. He proposed to help them by taking them one by one in his beak to a lake nearby.

The fish agreed, and the heron started taking them one by one, except he was eating them as he took them. The crab understood what was going on and he asked the heron to save him also; but smartly he jumped on his neck and bit him, till he let go. So the fish and other animals were safe."

The birds agreed the crow was right. But the owl was not very happy about the story.

So to listen to it the crow said, "Have you heard the story of the lamb and the wise man?" Birds wanted to hear.

The crow said, "There was a wise man that had received from a farmer a goat. He placed the goat on his back and started toward home. Three thieves started saying, "Look at that man going around with a very ugly and dirty animal on his back." The wise man was astonished, looked the goat over, yes, it was a goat. He put it back on his shoulders and the three thieves continued saying, "look, a pig on his shoulder, he smells so much." The wise man did not know what to think, he thought maybe his sight was not so good. So he dropped the goat that ran away. The thieves caught him and ate him."

The owl was offended and flew away. The other birds and the crow decided it was better not to have a king.

CHAPTER 4

A REMEDY AGAINST PAIN

A butterfly was flying from one flower to another, when she heard someone crying. That's strange, she thought, she got scared and broke her wings by hitting a young lemon tree.

"Ah, what is going to happen now? I cannot fly and I will die of sadness."

While complaining she remembered the cry that she had heard and asked the wind. "Who was crying before me?"

"I am a naked stem without a flower, the wind made me blind. What is a stem without a flower."?

The butterfly crawled next to him and said, "You are not the only one suffering. My wings are broken, I cannot longer fly in the air."

The stem stayed quiet and thought, but he was quiet for so long, that the butterfly was getting very nervous.

Finally he said, "We can help each other. Lay on me, so that your wings are in the wind and I be a flower again."

The butterfly smiled. The birds came to help them; they put the butterfly on the green stem.

From then on they are butterfly that fly and others that are changed in flower so that the stems can cradle.

CHAPTER 5

THE WIZARD CALLED JOHN

Once upon a time lived a very poor miller with 5 children, four boys and one girl that was always complaining.

One day someone knocked at the door, it was a very old man, "I am tired and hungry, can you help me?"

The miller's wife gave him some bread and the best chair in the house. After the old man had eaten and slept, while leaving he said, "I am a wizard, and you were so kind that I would like to repay you."

So he started asking first to the oldest boy what he wanted.

He said he wanted to get as big as his dad and go and look for fortune. The second wanted a magic wand to do his homework. The third wanted a palace full of gold coins so he could buy all the sweets in the world, the fourth one a lot of cats with a long tail so he could pull them. The wizard did not know what to say to these strange requests. Then it was the little girl turn.

"I have very sweet eyes. I want them sweeter so that when every morning my brothers take milk, it will be so sweet like mommy had placed a lot of sugar in these cups."

The wizard heard these words, smiled and said, "I will give your wish and send fortune to this house."

From then on they were no longer poor.

CHAPTER 6

WHY ARE CROWS BLACK

Many centuries ago, when the earth and people had just been created, all the crows were white like the snow.

In these times, people did not have horses, or guns, or iron weapons, but they had enough food by hunting buffalos.

The crows were friends of the buffalos and made everything very hard for the humans. They would fly and when they saw the humans coming, they would go to the buffalos and warn them.

"Craw, craw, cousins, the hunters are coming, they are behind that hill. Be careful." And the buffalos would run away, and people were starving.

The people got together trying to come up with some ideas.

From all the crows, there was one that was the biggest of them all. This crow was their guide.

An old and wise man said, "We must catch the big white crow, and teach him a lesson, or we will make him starve to death."

He took a large buffalo skin with still the head and the horns attached to it. This skin was placed on the back of a very courageous young man, and was told to go where the buffalos roamed.

"They will think that you are one of them, so catch the white crow."

The young man joined the other buffalos. No one was paying attention to him. When the hunters came out ready with their arrows, the crows arrived warning the buffalos.

"Run, run, cousins, the hunters are coming to kill you. Be careful of the arrows."

The buffalos ran away, except for the fake one, he kept on eating.

The big white crow came down, landing on the hunter's shoulder, and said, "Are you deaf, brother, run. The hunters are coming; they are right behind the hill. Save yourself."

But the young man caught the crow by the paws.

He placed it around his neck, so that the crow could not fly away.

The people sat around and said, "What can we do with this bad bird that he was making us starve?"

"Let's burn him!", answered the hunter, and before they could stop him, he placed the crow in the fire, rope, stone and all.

"Now, he will learn his lesson," he said.

The rope burned, and the big crow was able to fly away from the fire, but some of his feathers had become black from the fire.

"Craw, craw, I promise I will never again give the alarm. I promise."

The crow flew away, but from that point on they were all black.

CHAPTER 7

PETER AND THE COW

In a small village lived a son and his mother and were very poor. Peter was very young and he had to work all day but he also made brooms to sell at the market. Every day he took his cow in the field, and the cow will give fresh milk.

One morning, Peter decided to make new brooms, and followed by the cow kept walking in the woods. He got tired and decided to rest for awhile. He laid down on the grass and saw many elves that were happily singing and playing.

"You are lucky. You are playing and I have to work all day and do not have time to play and have fun."

"Come and play with us."

"Oh, thank you, and what are you playing?"

"Soccer, you go and guard the door."

So they started playing. Everything was just fine till the soccer ball hit the boy in the face and for five minutes he could not see anything.

The elves were laughing and running around.

When Peter finally could see, he could not find his cow and thought she was lost in the woods.

He went back home and told his mother what had happened.

The next day both mother and son went to look for the cow, and finally after a long time they found her dead. The mother was desperate, no cow, no milk.

Time went by, and one morning Peter was making more brooms when he saw two elves with a cow.

Peter looked and noticed that it was his cow. So he jumped on her back, but the cow did not like that and she started running in the field with the two elves attached to her tail.

The cow ran and ran and arrived next to a lake, and finally jumped in the water. The boy started saying his last prayers when he saw at the bottom of the lake a palace made out of crystal.

He went in and saw many ladies and cavaliers. A king approached him.

"You took my cow," said the boy.

"No, my dear boy, this is my cow, the two elves sold it to me."

The boy started saying his whole story, and the king, who was a good and wise man, proposed to give the boy a purse full of gold coins in exchange for the cow that was giving good milk.

"No, that it is not right, give me back my cow, so I can give it back to my mother, and I will leave."

The king was astonished for that refusal and said, "How can you refuse such an offer, I need the cow. With his milk we can drink tea properly."

"I need it more, because we are very poor."

The king was taken by his honesty, gave back the cow and also a purse full of gold coins.

But the boy refused, "They will think that I have stolen the coins. Keep them, please."

"I don't feel right. Here is a proposal; every day around five o'clock bring me a bucket of milk and I will pay you." said the king.

Peter was happy, told to mother what had happened, and the mother thought the boy was crazy. So he took her by the lake, and there were two elves bringing a purse full of golden coins.

Peter was honest and his honesty had been rewarded, and now he could live happily with his mother.

CHAPTER 8

A PROOF OF LOVE

There was a king with a beautiful daughter that every one admired for her beauty and kindness.

Many would come offering gold, jewels in order to marry her. But the young girl could not make up her mind.

"Who will be my groom?" she would ask her father.

"I don't know. You choose, I am sure that you will make a good choice."

"Okay, then tell everyone that a very poisonous snake has bitten me. I am dead. Every members of the royal family will wear black. Play funeral music, and let see what happens."

The king was surprised, did not care for the idea, but he went along anyway.

The sad news went around. The villagers were sad, old women were praying. The pretenders came and asked for their jewels and gold back.

"Your daughter is dead, so give me back my gold."

The king was disgusted but gave them back their gold. Now he knew why the daughter had done this.

Finally a poor young man came. He was crying away, and said, "Sire, I have heard of this terrible news and I cannot find peace. I am bringing robes for her, I loved her in secret, because I did not feel I was good enough for her. I want for her to be the most beautiful in the tomb. Please also put this food next to her for her voyage in the unknown."

The king was very touched by this act. He went to the balcony, told every one to be quiet and said, "I have good news, my daughter is not dead. I wanted a proof of love from all her suitors. Now I know who really loves my daughter. Is this young man, poor but sincere."

They married and she was the happiest girl in the Kingdome.

CHAPTER 9

EYES UP
BY
PATRICIA C. WILLS

Eyes up!
Leg on!
Two more strides
Just one left
Gather up
Air borne
Cold, clear air
Two bodies as one
Ears forward—what's next?
Eyes forward—trust me!
Landing!
Gather up—change leads!
Are you still with me?
Yes! Surge forward
I'm ready for the next challenge!
Just go! We are free!
Don't look back!
There is a whole field
Just for us
Are you game?
Eyes up! Ears forward! Air borne

CHAPTER 10

FALLING FROM THE DONKEY

One day a good man was riding his donkey, he passed a small garden, saw a branch that was over the gate full of pears. He was dying to have some pears, so he rose up a little bit from the saddle, grabbed the branch with one hand, and with the other one tried to grab the biggest pear. But he could not; the donkey got scared and started galloping away.

The man tried not to fall so he grabbed the branch with both hands.

While he was hanging from the branch, the gardener came and started yelling, "Hey you, what are you doing to my tree?"

"My friend, you may not believe me, but I fell from my donkey."

The gardener could not believe that you could fall up, instead of down, took his stick and beat him.

Be careful there are different ways to fall from a donkey.

CHAPTER 11

THE BIG ELEPHANT

At the beginning of the world, the elephant was as tall as the other animals, but he was very demanding and wanted everyone to serve him as he was the king.

The people in the savannah were tired of his behavior, so they secretly met to discuss what to do.

"We are tired of this elephant, we are living in terror, we keep protesting but nothing happens. It is time to stop him and do something about his behavior."

They discussed for a long time, and then they decided to teach him a lesson. They invited the elephant to a banquet, so they could keep him occupied.

The elephant accepted, he was happy on how well they were treating him. While he was busy eating, all the other animals got around him and started hitting him with their horns, their paws, till the elephant was bloated from head to feet.

The poor elephant crawled to the river and jumped in to take care of the wounds on his body.

It took many days to get well, and he finally was well, he looked at his body in the river and noticed that it was big, heavy, only the ears were the same, and looked really strange.

He had become the biggest animal in the savannah, but his power had ended.

He couldn't command anymore animals smaller than him because he remembered the lesson he had received, so if you notice, the elephant always walks with his head down, ashamed of himself.

CHAPTER 12

WHY PEOPLE DIE

Long time ago the moon, which dies and rebirths every four weeks, told the rabbit. "Tell all men that if I can die and come back again, they can also die and come back".

Unfortunately the rabbit became confused and instead he said to the people, "Because when I die, I don't come back, the same will happen to you."

When the rabbit went back to the moon, he said, "I told them that when I die I will not come back, and the same will be for all of them."

"Why did you say that?" yelled the moon. She threw a stick to the rabbit and broke his hip.

The rabbit ran away, and forever with a broken hip.

And men die and do not come back.

CHAPTER 13

THE UNGRATEFUL LION

Many years ago, in a small village lived a lion. He was a nuisance, scaring everyone and killing anyone coming next to his hut.

The village's king got all his hunters together and they decided to look for the lion and kill him.

They made a very strong hut, so they could place the lion in there before killing him. The hunters caught the lion and locked him in while thinking how to punish him.

The next day, a man was passing by, and the lion implored him to open the door and let him go. The man first was hesitant, but he then opened the door. As soon as the lion was out he jumped on the man trying to kill him. The man pleaded but in vain.

The people informed the villagers of what had happened.

The man and the lion reported different facts, many said to kill the man, others to spare him.

A wolf came by, listening to the different facts.

The man told the wolf that the lion was suffering, and had begged him to open the door. But the lion tried to kill him as soon as he was out.

The wolf listened attentively.

The wolf was smart and wise, and he asked for a demonstration. He went to the hut to verify the place.

The man entered in, opened the door, and the lion went in. The wolf asked them to place the door in the original position. The man and the lion testified that the door was shut. The man went out and closed the door so the lion could not come out.

The wolf talked to the lion and said, "You are ungrateful, the man was trying to help you, and you tried to kill him. So you will remain locked in, till you die, and the man will go."

The man left, and the lion stayed in, suffering and paying for his wrong doings.

CHAPTER 14

THE LYING IRISHMAN

Way in the East lived a king that had only one daughter. When she became older, the king said that she will marry only the person that would be able to have him say three times "it is a lie, it is a lie, it is a lie."

The news spread around the world, all the way to Ireland where a poor widow lived with a son that was famous for his lies. One evening the boy returned home, and said, "I would be surprised if I would not marry the princess, bless me mother, because tomorrow I am leaving."

The next day he left, he travelled for a long time and finally arrived to the royal castle. At the door he was stopped by the guards.

"Where do you think you are going, small Irishman?"

"I am going to your king to marry his daughter," answered the liar.

The guards took him to the king. The king took him to a big field, where his sheep and his herd were grazing, and asked him "What do you think of my sheep?"

"What sheep? These are herd, it is nothing. You should see my mother's sheep," said the liar.

"Why are they so special?" asked the king.

"Well, they are huge, and underneath one of the cabbages you can have a wedding banquet."

"Uhm, uhm," said the king, and then took the boy to his large garden, where he was cultivating beans. He asked, "What do you think of my beans?"

"What I think? They are nothing, you should see the ones in my mother's garden." said the Irish liar.

"Why are they special?"

"Why? They are so tall that they can reach the clouds. One time I was collecting the beans and I kept going up and up till I reached the clouds, from there I saw a house and a flea. Because I needed a new bag, I killed the flea, took her skin and made myself a new bag, then I climbed down, the leaves broke under my feet. The whole stem broke. I fell and I was between two rocks, I could not get out, I took the knife from my pocket, cut my head off, and send it home to tell my family what had happened. During the voyage my head saw a wolf. She took my head and ran away. I was annoyed by this, so I jumped behind her, and I caught the wolf, I cut her tail off with my knife. And on her tail it was written that your father had been my father's servant."

The king screamed, "That's a lie, that's a lie, that's a lie."

"I know," said the Irishman, "but you asked for, and now you have to give me your daughter in marriage,"

And that it is how a poor Irishman boy married the kings' daughter.

CHAPTER 15

THE MONKEY AND THE TURTLE

The turtle was very bored; every day was the same. The sea went forever, and there was one wave after another. No one ever came to make him happy, except one time when a whale and a group of dolphins had come by.

One day, the turtle saw a monkey eating away a bunch of bananas.

"Why look for a friend in the sea?" thought the turtle. "The monkey, looks like an ideal companion, certainly more friendly than a crab."

"Good morning, monkey. Do you want to be my friend?"

"Good morning turtle, certainly."

From that day on, they spend time together, and the turtle had never been so happy.

One day the monkey asked him to taste the bananas, and promised to teach him how to climb trees.

In the evening, the monkey told everything to his wife. "I had fun, you should see how well the turtle could climb the tree. He is my best friend."

Also the turtle told his wife, "What a wonderful friend. I was so bored before I met him."

But his wife did not agree, she thought, "my husband is always with his new friend. I need to get rid of that terrible monkey."

One evening, the turtle find his wife in bed. "Are you sick?"

"Yes, very sick, the doctor said that I am about to die, and the only way to save me is for me to eat a monkey's heart."

"A monkey's heart? But where can I find It.? The only monkey I know is my friend."

"Then, I am going to die," said the wife.

The turtle was desperate, he thought and then he decided to sacrifice his friend.

He slowly walked to his friend's house.

"Good morning turtle, how nice to see you, what it is going on?"

"My wife would like to invite you to dinner, this evening, can you come?"

"Of course, I can."

The monkey followed his friend all the way to the river, but could not go on, because he did not know how to swim.

"Jump on my shell, I will carry you."

The monkey jumped on his shell. Then he said, "You seem very sad, what it is going on, you know I would do anything for you."

"Ah, my friend, my wife is dying and the only way to save her is if she eats your heart."

"Ah," the monkey thought, but there is a limit. How can I resolve this? I could drown anytime.

Then he said, "It is terrible, I would gladly give you my heart, but we need to go back and take it."

"Your heart is not in your chest?"

"What? Don't you know, that we monkey keep our heart in a vase, next to our house, before we go somewhere?"

The turtle stopped and said, "So what do we do?"

"Simple, take me back and I will give you my heart."

The turtle went back, the monkey jumped off and climbed the tree.

"Wow, I am safe. You scared me."

"But what happened to the heart that you promised me.?"

"The heart? You are not very smart. It is in my chest and I am keeping it. Goodbye".

The turtle went back home, he said, he had lost his friend, but his wife seemed to be cured.

CHAPTER 16

BOB AND THE ROBIN

The old grouchy cat was walking along the water and saw between the bushes Robert, the Red tail Robin.

"Where are you going?" the cat asked.

"To the king, I want to sing for him," said the robin.

"Come here, come here, I want to show you this beautiful white circle that I have around my neck."

"No, not now, eat your little mouse, but you are not catching me."

And Robert flew away. He finally arrived at an old bush, and on this old bush there was an old hawk called Eat Everything.

"Where are you going Bob?."

"To the king, I want to sing for him", he answered.

"Come here, come here, I want to show you the beautiful plumage that I have."

"No, I am not coming, go ahead and eat the lark, but I am flying away."

He kept flying till arrived to a canyon, and there was a fox.

"Where are you going," the fox asked.

"To the king, to sing a beautiful song."

"Come here, closer, I want to show you the beautiful mark that I have on my tail."

"No, I am not coming near you. Go ahead and eat the lamb, but me, I am flying away."

He kept flying, flying, till he arrived to a river, and on the bank there was a young boy.

"Where are you going?" The young boy asked.

"To the king, to sing a beautiful song."

"Come, come, in my pocket I have beautiful little stones that I want to give you."

"No, thank you, go ahead and catch the lark. Me, you are not catching"

The small robin flew away, and finally arrived at the royal palace. He went on the balcony and started singing. The king was listening, then he asked the queen." What can we give him after that beautiful song?"

"Let's give him in marriage the little finch."

And so they did, Robin married and everyone danced. After a while he went away with his bride to a bush and there he lived happily ever after.

CHAPTER 17

YEN AND YANG

Yen and her husband Yang, a wonderful archer lived during the emperor Yak. Yang was one of the Imperial guards and could really use his arc and arrows.

One day the emperor decided to call Yang and asked him to eliminate some of the suns and save the people. In the sky had appeared 10 suns, people were so hot and the dryness lasted for many years.

Yang used his ability and eliminate nine of them, only one was left. He became very famous, and the Mother Queen called from far away, wanted to give him a pill of immortality, but also told him, "Don't take the pill right away, first you must pray for 12 months and do not eat."

He was smart and decided to follow the rules. He started preparing and took the pill at home. Unfortunately he had just been called for an urgent mission, so he left. While he was gone, Yen noticed a light and a sweet odor coming from the comer of the room. She saw the pill, and could not resist taking it. As soon as she took the pill she became very light, she could fly. She heard her husband coming and she flew out the window.

Yang with his arrows followed her in the sky, but a strong wind brought him back to the house. Yen flew right to the moon, she was so tired that she spit the pill, the pill changed into a rabbit of wade, while Yen changed in a toad with three legs.

From then on she lives on the moon and throws back the arrows that the husband sends.

Yang build a palace on the sun, so they could see each other every fifteen days in the month. They both represent the sun and the moon, the positive and the negative, the darkness and the light, the feminine and masculine, the duality that governs the universe.

CHAPTER 18

HEAVEN AND HELL

After a very long and courageous life, a very valiant samurai died and he was destined for Heaven.

He was a very curious person and he asked if he could see what was like in Hell. The angel decided to show him.

He found himself in a very big room. In the center there was a table covered with different food. But the people seating at the table, were very thin and almost all bones.

"How is it possible?" He asked the angel.

"Look at all that food."

"They have forks and spoon, but they are very long, and so they have to be careful how they handle them and to be able to put food in their mouth."

The samurai was scared.

What a punishment, they couldn't eat.

He asked to be taken to Heaven.

The Heaven had the same big room like hell. There was a big table with all kind of food, and many people sitting around.

These people had the same long stick that was in Hell but they could eat. The only difference was that this people were happy and well fed.

"How is this possible?" asked the surprised samurai.

The angel smiled. "In Hell every one has to work very hard to get the food to their mouth, because this is how they behaved in life, only thinking about themselves. Here instead each one feeds the person next to them, so they can all eat."

Heaven and Hell are in your hands, behave accordingly.

CHAPTER 19

THE FOX AND THE DUCK

A fox had captured a beautiful and fat duck that was sleeping next to the water.

The duck was screeching and whistling, and the fox was laughing.

"Go ahead, but what would you do if our parts were reversed?"

"Well," the duck said," it is easy, I will put my hands together, close my eyes, and pray thanking that I was able to eat you."

The fox put her hands together, closed his eyes and said a thank you prayer.

While doing this, the duck opened her wings and flew away from the water.

The fox made himself a promise. Never pray for thanking till you have food in your stomach.

CHAPTER 20

THE MOUSE AND THE CAT

The little mouse went to visit the cat. There she was outside the house, purring away.

The mouse said, "What are you doing, my dear friend, what are you doing, my dear friend?"

And the cat, "I am making little socks and gloves for when it is going to be cold."

The mouse," I hope they last for a long time, a very long time."

The cat, "They will last, they will last, till they break."

The mouse, "Yesterday I swept my little house, just yesterday."

The cat, "So it is clean, so it is clean, my dear mouse."

The mouse, "I found a coin, I found a coin made of silver."

The cat, "So, now you are rich, so now you are rich, my dear and pretty little mouse."

The mouse, "I went to the market with the silver coin, I went to the market."

The cat, "So you gave yourself a nice walk, a very nice walk."

The mouse, "I bought some hot bread, very sweet hot bread with the coin."

The cat, "Then I wish you a good appetite, a good appetite indeed."

The mouse, "I placed the bread on the window, right on the window."

The cat, "By now it should be cool to eat, I am sure it is good to eat."

The mouse, "A cat ate my hot bread, yes a cat ate it."

The cat, "And now I will eat you, yes, I will eat you, and you will go well with my bread."

And so saying, the cat jumped on the little mouse and ate it.

CHAPTER 21

THE HISTORY OF MIAMI BEACH

Many year ago, there was a terrible drought, all the trees died, the lakes were dry, and the sun's rays were so hot that they shined night and day.

In a small village, there was a family. The mother's name was Rose, she was forty years old and lived with her son Mark who was fourteen years old.

They rented a field, but after paying for the rent there was almost nothing left. So Mark would collect wood and herbs and sell it at the market. He was a very nice young man, always ready to help others. He liked all the children and his best friend was Paul.

One day, early in the morning, he went as usual to get herbs, while walking he was thinking, "My good friend Paul told me yesterday that John, a very rich man needs herbs to give to his horse, so let me cut a lot of herbs and sell them to him."

While thinking, he did not realize that he had reached what was called the Unknown Zone.

At this place during spring, there were many fishes, shrimps and herbs, but now it was full of stones. Mark sighed, and decided to go to another place when he saw a white figure behind a temple. He was surprised and thought, "Must be a white rabbit."

Thinking that rabbits will eat good herbs, he followed it. At the end of the valley the rabbit disappeared, but at the same time Mark saw a large field of herbs. He was very happy, so he started filling his basket.

The next day he returned and strangely enough the herbs had re grown again, and this happened two days in a row. So he thought, "Why don't I take these and plant them behind my house, so instead of coming here every day, I can just go behind my house and get them". So he started digging these herbs. While doing so, he saw a puddle of water, and on the surface a beautiful pearl. Mark took it and placed it in his pocket, and then went home with a basket full of herbs.

When he got home, the sun was going down, and his mother was preparing soup.

When she saw the boy, she said, "Why are you so late coming home? I was worried."

Mark told her the whole thing and showed her the pearl. The pearl was shining so much that they could not keep the eyes open. So the mom took the pearl and hided it in a vase full of rice.

After dinner, Mark planted the herbs behind the house next to the bamboos.

The next day, he was up early, went to the garden but all the herbs were dried out. He went back in the house to see if the pearl was still there. He opened the vase and yelled, "Mom, Mom, come and see this"

The vase was full of rice and on top the pearl. They understood that the pearl was magic, as they kept placing it in the vase more rice would appear, and if they placed silver in the vase and the pearl on top of it, more silver would appear. So now Mark and his mom had plenty money to buy food and clothes. And when their neighbors had no food, the mom would bring them rice and money. But soon the news spread around, and when the rich man, John, heard it, told his men, "You must get me that pearl."

His man said, "Sir, they are poor, maybe we can buy it from them."

But John did not want to do it that way, so he told them to go to Rose's house, and tell her that it was his pearl, and if they did not return it, they will go to jail.

When Paul heard of what was planned, he went to Rose and Mark's house, told them to run away. While mother and son were busy preparing a suitcase, John came to the door and said, "Give me back my pearl, or you both are going to die." Mark got angry and pointing the finger at the man said, "How can you accuse me of theft, you hate poor people."

The man did not answer but told the servants to look all over the house, but nothing was found. While they were searching, Mark took the pearl and swallowed it.

The servants started kicking him and beating him. Mark fainted. Neighbors came to help and send the servants away, took Mark in their house to take care of him.

Rose, was sitting next to her son, crying away.

Midnight came, Mark woke up and said, "I am thirsty, please give me some water."

The mom happily gave him water. Mark kept asking for more, he could not wait any more for water, so he took a bucket and drank all of it. His mother was terrified.

"Son, what is wrong, I have never seen you drinking so much water."

"I don't know, mom, I feel like I have fire inside, and I am so thirsty."

"I have no more water to give you,"

"I will go to the lake so I can drink."

It was raining, he did not care. He went to the river and started drinking, half of the river went dry.

"What is happening, my son?"

Mark turned around, he had changed, and he had two horns on his head, blue hair around his mouth and red scales around his neck.

"Let me go, mother, I want to be a dragon so that I can vindicate myself."

Under the thunders the water was up again.

John, the rich man, arrived just in time with his servants carrying torches, he wanted to open Mark's stomach and take the pearl.

Mark saw them coming.

He jumped in the river and waves as high as the sky came out.

"Old woman, where is your son?" said John, shacking Rose's shoulders.

"You are a bad man. Go to the river. Son here is your enemy."

John kicked Rose on the ground, ran to the river. A huge wave took John and his servants and drowned them.

The wind and the rain stopped. The sky was now clear.

Mark came out from the river and said, "Mom, I am leaving."

"Son, when are you coming back?"

"I will not be back till the rocks will come out, and the horses will have horns."

Rose was crying away, "Oh, my son, Oh, my son."

Mark looked up. Twenty four times, she called him and twenty four times he raised his head. At every time, sand would come up, and Miami's beach was born.

CHAPTER 22

THE RIVER AND THE HORSE

A little horse lived with his mother and never walked away from her.

One day the mother said, "You need to start going out by yourself, so take this small package to the windmill."

Taking the sack on his back, and happy to be useful the colt went towards the windmill.

On the way there he saw a river, and thought, "What should I do, should I cross it?"

He could not make up his mind, and there was no one around to ask for advice. He finally saw a cow that was browsing.

The colt approached him, "Uncle, can I cross the river?"

"Of course you can, it is not very deep, look it gets to my knees. Don't worry."

The colt started galloping, then a squirrel approached him, "Don't go, it is dangerous, you will drown."

"But, is it not really deep," said the confused colt.

"Yesterday one of my friend drowned," said the squirrel.

The colt did not know what to do, so he went home to his mother.

"I came back because the river is too deep, I cannot cross it."

"Are you sure?. I don't think it is too deep," said the mother.

"That's what the cow told me, but the squirrel kept insisting that the river is dangerous, and one of his friends had just died crossing it."

"My son, think. The cow is big and of course he thinks that the river is not very deep, the squirrel is small. He could drown in a small pond."

The colt listened to his mother and went back to the river sure of himself.

When the squirrel saw him, he said, "Have you decided to drown?"

"I am going to cross it."

Then the colt discovered that the river was not as deep as the cow had told him, and not as deep as the squirrel had told him.

CHAPTER 23

THE EAGLE AND THE WREN

The eagle and the wren wanted to see who could fly higher that the other one. The winner will be the king of all birds.

The wren went first, the eagle followed him, went pass him, and made big circles in the sky.

The wren was tired, so the eagle passed him, so the wren quietly sat on the eagles' back.

At the end, the eagle was getting also tired and asked, "Where are you wren?"

"I am here, higher than you."

So the wren had won the competition.

CHAPTER 24

THE CAMEL AND THE ANT

A camel was walking thru the desert, when he saw a small ant in the grass. The little ant was carrying a big straw, ten times her weight. The camel looked for a while and then said, "The more I am looking at you, and the more I admire you. You are carrying a weight ten times your size, and here I am carrying nothing and my knees are bending. How is it possible?"

"How?" Answered the ant, stopping for awhile. "It is easy, I am working for myself while you are working for your owner."

The ant took the straw back and kept on walking.

CHAPTER 25

THE VANE GIRAFFE

In Africa, lived a beautiful giraffe, fast and thin, and taller than any other animals. She knew everyone admired her, so she did not respect anyone, and never helped any one. In fact she went around saying, "Look at me, I am gorgeous."

The other animals were tired of hearing this, and they made fun of her, but she did not listen, she was so occupied with herself.

One day, a monkey decided to teach her a lesson, so he approached her and said, "You are so beautiful, so tall, taller than anyone," and took her to a palm tree in the forest.

When they got there, the monkey asked the giraffe to get him some dates that were growing on the top, and that were the sweetest.

The giraffe tried, tried but could not reach the dates. The monkey jumped on her back, then on her neck and finally was able to reach the dates. When he climbed down he told the giraffe," You see my dear, you may be the tallest one, the most beautiful one, but you cannot live without other people's help, you need all of us."

The giraffe learned the lesson and from then on, she worked with the other animals and respected them.

CHAPTER 26

THE FOX AND THE ROOSTER

One day, the fox and the rooster were talking. "How many tricks do you know?" asked the fox.

"I know three," said the rooster. "And how many do you know?."

"I know at least seventy three," answered the fox.

"That many? Tell me one."

"Well, my grandfather told me to close one eye and scream very loudly."

"That's it," said the rooster, "I can do that too."

So the rooster closed one eye and gave out a loud scream.

But the eye that he had closed was the one next to the fox, so the fox took him by the neck and ran away.

A good woman saw the rooster and started screaming, "Let that rooster go, he is mine."

The rooster whispered to the fox, "Tell her that I belong to you'"

The fox opened the mouth, and the rooster fell out of it.

Quickly the rooster flew on the house's roof, and with one closed eye, he got out a loud scream.

CHAPTER 27

THE GENIES OF THE FIREPLACE

Once upon a time there was a couple without children that fought all the times. One day Mary, the wife, after she had been beaten by her husband decided to run away. She met another man and married him.

The husband, Paul, after many adversities, he had lost his job and went begging in the street. One day he was looking for food and money and fainted in front of Mary. She recognized him and offered him food and shelter. The man took advantage of her kindness, he had not recognized as being his ex wife. When was the time for her second husband to come home, she did not want for the two to meet, so she asked the beggar to hide underneath a sheet of straw.

When her second husband, James, came home, he decided to burn the straw so he could have ashes to pour in his rice's field.

When Mary saw the flames, she felt so guilty to have caused her ex-husband death, and she threw herself in the flames.

Paul had been able to escape the flames,

And watched his wife die, and without hesitation he threw himself in the flames so the two could be reunited in Heaven.

But it was not the end, a servant came, saw the two bodies tried to save them and he went to close to the flames, and he also died.

From then on, the three genies of the fireplace get together; the two stones (Mary and Paul) sustain the pot of the flame represented by their servant.

CHAPTER 28

THE CARPENTER AND THE TRUNK

One day the Emperor went to the carpenter, the poorest in his entire kingdom, and said, "I would like for you to build me a trunk where I can place all my treasures."

The poor carpenter was so happy for this honor, he could not believe it.

"Yes," the Emperor said, "I want for you to build me one, and I can see from your reaction that you will do a good job. Only one thing I can tell you is that I will pay the first 250 dollars now, and in thirty days, when I come to collect it, other 250 dollars." And he left.

The carpenter, first stood there without believing, then he looked at his money in his hands. He was so happy that he decided to give a big party, and invited the whole village.

They all met, dancing, drinking and eating till the early morning of the next day.

The carpenter went to sleep; he awoke up pretty late, and decided to start working on the trunk. But he was so tired from the party and he went back to bed.

When he woke up the next day, he was reinvigorated. So he went in the woods to find the perfect tree for his wood. While walking he met a friend, he heard of the good news, and they decided to celebrate by going to the tavern. He met other friends and others and so on.

Now you can figure out that days had gone by between parties, drinking. On the 29'th day, the carpenter was still at the tavern drinking, when he suddenly remembered that the next day the emperor was coming to his house to get the trunk. So he left and ran home.

He was so drunk that he went the wrong way, and he came up the river, and in the middle what did he see? A large piece of wood, beautiful, but old. He put it on his shoulders, all happy and took it home. He worked all night, rasping it, cleaning. At sunrise he stopped and he saw that he had built a beautiful and strong trunk. He was so happy. He went to sleep.

The next morning the emperor knocked at the door. When he saw the trunk, his face became very white. "Carpenter, I was right. This trunk is fantastic. Tell me what you wish and you will have it in addition to your money."

The carpenter was so happy and answered, "Nothing, sire, your happiness is enough for me."

CHAPTER 29

THE DONKEY AND THE TIGER

One day a donkey and a hungry tiger met on an iced river. The donkey saw what the tiger's intentions were. He was planning to eat him.

So he talked to him, "Noble tiger, I see you are hungry, I am proposing you a pact. If you can reach the other side of the river before me, you can eat me, otherwise I can leave."

The tiger accepted, she was sure to win. And she did. She was very satisfied, and said, "Okay donkey, I won, and now I will eat you."

"But you know why I was late?" Asked the donkey. "While I was running, I also was writing on the ice."

The tiger looked, and yes, he noticed scratches and hoof steps. Since she did not know how to write, nor read, she thought that they were letter. She looked at the donkey again, impressed by the donkey's wisdom.

The donkey was not happy about this, and he emitted a long hee haw, and explained that she knew how to sing. The tiger was really impressed and said, "my dear donkey, I am not going to eat you. I like to become your friend. You can come and live with me. I will get some of your wisdom and you are under my protection."

The donkey accepted and followed the tiger.

One day the tiger told the donkey. "I am going hunting, and I have to leave you by yourself for few minutes. But don't worry, if someone comes to you, sing and I will come and save you." And she left.

The donkey starting browsing the grass next to the tiger place, and she was so happy that she could not keep emitting a long heehaw.

As soon as the tiger heard it, she ran to her friend, "Is everything all right?" The donkey was sorry, and said, "Forgive me, my dear tiger. I was so happy that I started singing."

The tiger smiled, but she was a little annoyed, "That's okay, but next time be careful. I am going back to hunt."

The donkey remained by himself, kept on eating the grass, but he was so pleased by the kindness of the tiger that he again let out a heehaw.

The tiger ran again to save him, "Is someone bothering you?"

The donkey was really embarrassed, "l am sorry, I did it again."

The tiger was becoming more and more nervous, "Be careful my friend, or next time I will not come."

The donkey asked forgiveness, and the tiger left.

But again another hee haw. The tiger was busy chasing a prey, thought of a false alarm, and did not go.

Pity, because this time the donkey had been attacked by wolves. He was devoured by the wolves, not even a bone was left behind.

CHAPTER 30

ELIZABETH'S QUESTIONS

Bud decided to go for a long trip and find fortune. He arrived to China and went to Beijing to meet with the king who was supposed to be wise and nice.

The king, while he was surrounded by love and respect from his people, was very sad.

His daughter, a princess, was beautiful, smart, cultured and refined, but very cruel. Many had come for her hand, and she had scorned every men. She had decided that she would marry only the one that would answer correctly to her three questions. But if the answers were not right, they will be put to death.

The king tried to deter the young men to come, but she was so beautiful that they would not listen and had died.

When Bud came to Beijing, he knew the story, and could not resist seeing her. He became enchanted with the girl and decided to try. The king tried to dissuade him but to not avail.

The court was all together to see what would happen.

The princess started, "What is the creature that lives everywhere, is friendly to everyone and does not tolerate anyone that is the same as her."

"Princess, it is the sun." Answered Bud.

The answer was right.

The princess again," Who is the mother that has children but she eats them when they are grown."

Bud answered quickly," The sea, the currents go back in the sea that is where they start from"

The princess was surprised so were the court people of the wisdom of the young man.

Now the last question," Which is the tree whose leaves are white on one side but black on the other side,"

"This tree is the year, with days and nights."

The emperor was so happy; finally no more young man will die. The two married and lived happily ever after.

CHAPTER 31

THE THREE DAUGHTERS

One upon a time there was a man with only one daughter. One morning he woke up in good spirit and decided to go for a walk. He told his daughter not to leave the house and he went. While whistling and walking, he met a man, very polite that said, "Hello, old man. I wish you a good day. I saw your daughter and I think she is beautiful. Can I marry her?"

The man felt good about the compliments, and said, "Sure, young man. My daughter will be very happy to marry you. Come tonight and you can take her with you."

They smiled and they went their own ways.

The man kept on walking and whistling, and he met another young man also very polite.

"Hello, old man. I hope the sun never leaves you. I love your daughter, can I marry her?"

The man knew he shouldn't say yes, but he was too polite so he said, "Sure young man, come tonight and we will take care of every thing."

He walked again and met a third young man he was also eager to marry his daughter. And again he could not say no.

The evening arrived. The man did not know what to do, locked his daughter in the stable with a donkey and a dog. He hoped to come up with something. While thinking the first boy came in. They talked for a while, but then the young man asked where his bride to be was. The father, did not know what to do, he went to the stable to take his daughter, but when he entered instead of the donkey and the dog there were two more beautiful girls.

Now he had three daughters. Now he could keep his promises.

"I am really lucky," he thought. He took one girl and took her to the first young man. They hugged and left.

Then the second boy came in. The man gave him something to drink and eat, and then he went to get the second girl. The boy was so happy, thanked him, and left with his bride to be.

The third one comes, and the same thing repeated.

Years went by and the old man, was about to die, and he wanted to see his three daughters and their spouses. So he went to visit them. First went to the house of the first young man. They hugged, kissed, ate. After dinner, the young man said, that sometimes he did not know what to think about his wife, "She is really dear, but many times she does not listen to me, she is so stubborn, and is hard for her to get up from her chair."

The father thought, "Must be the donkey." He laughed and went to the second young man.

He was also happy but then took the father on one side and said, "I am happy for my wife, but many times she growls, and grinds her teeth. Sometimes she scares me." The father thought, "That must be the dog." He smiled and left.

Then he approached the third house.

The young man was sitting down, and his wife walked back and forth from the kitchen to bring food. They ate and then after dinner the young man said to his wife. "Wife go in the kitchen and get me a melon."

She silently obeyed, she came back with the melon, placed it on the table.

"Wife, not this one, bring me a bigger one".

The wife patiently left again, could not find any other melon and brought the same one, smiling.

And the father, thought, "Yes, this is my daughter, she knows what to do."

Now he had finally seen his daughter, he went back home and fell asleep.

CHAPTER 32

THE BOLD MAN

Once upon a time there was a king with seven daughters. They were tall and very pretty, but every night they left the castle without permission. The king was trying to find out where they went.

He had guards all around the castle, and couldn't understand why the girls would leave. So one day, he proclaimed, "Whoever tells me where my daughters are going, they can marry one of them and get a lot of money, but whoever stays in the castle for three nights and does not discover the secret of these outings will have his head cut off."

Many came, slept for the three nights, but nothing was discovered, the girls still went out, and the guys lost their heads.

One day a bold man, named Joseph, came and decided to resolve the problem. While he was going to the king, he met an old friend, a woman, and the old woman gave him a present. She gave him some tobacco and said when the girls want to leave in the night, they spray something in their room and everyone falls asleep, but if he sniffs the tobacco he will not.

He arrived at the palace, the king explained him the conditions. Joseph accepted and went to bed placing the tobacco under his nose and faked to fall asleep. At midnight the seven girls woke up and while they checked if Joseph was asleep, they dressed and left. Joseph followed them. The girls went in the garden and knocked three times to a big trunk tree and the tree opened a small door. Joseph did the same thing and he found himself in a garden with many trees covered with diamonds and branches covered with gold. The nightingales were singing and the ground was covered with grass and flowers. The sisters arrived to a large river and all boarded a beautiful boat where very handsome and tall men were. At sunrise they all left and Joseph ran before them so they could see he was still sleeping.

The second night the same thing happened. Joseph went to the king and showed him what was happening. The third morning the girls got up and asked for Joseph to be killed like everyone else. But the king, angry, told them what he had seen, and so they should be killed. He asked Joseph which one he wanted for wife. He choose the most beautiful one and smart one and became the king's son in law and later his successor.

CHAPTER 33

KIM'S RABBIT

Once upon a time there was a man named Kim. He was a very able business man. One day, he went walking in the woods, and he found two rabbits. He caught them and took them home. He told his wife to cook them for supper, since he also had a guest. He locked one rabbit in a sac and left the other one free in the house. The guest arrived, his name was David. Kim took the free rabbit and told him, "Go tell my wife to bring us the supper."

David was astonished. Kim opened the door and sat. Few minutes later his wife comes with the supper.

"Fantastic," said David. "That rabbit is formidable. I want it."

"it is very expensive," Kim said.

"I don't care; I will pay anything, just give me that rabbit."

Kim took the rabbit from the sac, and gave it to David.

"I cheated him," and he was so proud.

The next day David was working n the field, and tried his new rabbit.

"Go to my wife, and tell her to bring me my supper." And let the rabbit go.

Time came by, no rabbit, no wife. David went home and said to his wife. "Why did you not listen to the rabbit, and did not bring me my food, and where is the rabbit?"

The wife said, "He cheated you. Go to him and give him what he deserves".

David was very angry; he went to Kim's house.

From the window, Kim saw him, so he tied around his wife's neck the intestine of a bull full of wine and told his wife, "As soon as David comes thru that door to kill me, we will fake a fighting. I will throw you on the ground and fake that I am strangling you. The wine will look like blood. Then I will play this flute and you will make it look like you are being resuscitated. Understand?"

"Yes, I understand," said the wife.

Everything went like it was supposed to, and then David saw how powerful the flute was, and he forgot why he was there.

"Wow," he said, "with that flute I can kill my wife and resuscitate her. I want it. Give it to me, I will pay any amount of money."

Kim took his money, and gave him the flute. David went home anxious to try it.

He jumped on his wife and he strangled her. Then he used his flute. Nothing his wife was dead.

"He cheated me again," "This time no more tricks, I am going to kill him, so he will learn, and I'll throw him into the sea."

He was so angry, he was able to take Kim and place him in a sac. He took him at a top of a cliff, but before throwing him in, he went for a piece of wood, so he could beat him.

A shepherd came by with his sheep. He asked David why he was in the sac.

And David said, "If I stay in the sac, a rich man will come and will give me in marriage his beautiful daughter."

"I want her," the shepherd said, "Let's make a deal. I am going to give you my herd in exchange for me to stay in the sac."

They exchanged places. When the shepherd was well tied in, Kim left with his herd.

In the meantime David had found a piece of wood beat him and threw him the sea.

How surprised was he to see Kim with a herd in the city.

"How did you do it?" he asked.

"Easy," he lied. "While I was falling down I prayed the Gods that would save me and give me this herd, and here I am."

"What was the prayer; tell me so I can do the same thing. I will pay you well. Teach it to me."

Kim agreed to it, took David to the top of the hill, placed him in the sac, and pushed him down into the sea. He heard him praying, and then no more.

He went back to the city and thought, 'Man, I am really good at my job . . . no one can surpass me."

CHAPTER 34

THE BASIL'S GIRL

Once upon a time there was a poor girl that worked in the field and took care of the basil.

Every day a prince would come by, and laughing he would say, "Oh, girl with the basil, how many leaves does the basil have?"

And quickly she would answer, "Oh, you noble man, how many stars are in the sky?"

The prince would laugh and gallop away. With time the girl fell in love with the prince.

One day, after the usual talk, the prince said, "Dear girl, you will not see me for a while I am leaving for a battle to Lebbi."

The girl ran home, changed in a man's clothes, and ran to the city of Lebbi. She was there first, the prince arrived and the girl offered to play a game of chess, man to man.

"Gladly," said the prince. "If I loose I will give you my golden saber."

"Great, and if I loose, you will spend the night with one of my most beautiful slave."

They played two games, the first time the girl won, so she took the saber, the second was won by the prince. So during the night the girl changed her clothes to a slave and entered the prince's tend, and he did not know who she was.

After nine months, the girl had a beautiful baby boy. She had returned to her field and received the same visit from the prince, who had no idea that the baby was his.

One day, he told her, "Tomorrow, my dear, you will not see me, I am leaving for Tschini."

Like the previous times, the girl put some man's clothes on, and arrived before the prince to Tschini. She again proposed to play chess. The prince accepted, and said, "If you win, I will give you this beautiful golden watch."

"You are very generous, and if you win, I will let you have another beautiful slave."

The games handed, first the girl won, and got the watch then the prince won.

During the night the girl changed into a slave and entered the tent, and he did not know who she was.

After nine months another baby boy was born. The prince had no idea, and he kept coming by and talking to the girl.

Then one day he said, "My dear girl, tomorrow I am leaving for India."

Again the girl beat him to India, and again chess games.

The prince said, "I am so happy to see you, my dear friend, if this time you win I will give you a beautiful silk scarf"

"Thank you, my prince and me another beautiful slave"

The same thing repeated itself, and this time after nine months the girl had a beautiful baby girl. Years went by.

One day the prince said, "My dear girl, today I am getting married. I will have many guests. The bride is already at the castle, I better go or I will be late for my own wedding."

The girl, ran to her three children, now grown. The first, 9 years old, gave him the golden saber, the second, 8 years old, the golden watch, and the girl, 7 years old, the silken scarf. She sends them to the royal palace, and told them to sing a particular song.

When the three kids arrived at the royal castle, they all start singing, "As two princes we are going, with our sister, our little princess, to our father's wedding."

As he heard the song the prince ran out, and he saw the saber, the watch and the scarf and he immediately understood what had happened.

He turned towards his bride to be and said, "I will always respect you, but you see I have three children that I did not know about, therefore I need to marry their mother. I am sorry it was not our destiny to get married."

The bride to be was very angry and left the palace, the prince ran to the field to see the mother of his children.

"You, it is you,"

"Yes, me."

They went back to the castle, and they got married, and for forty days and nights there were festivities at the castle.

CHAPTER 35

THE MAGIC RING

There was a young man, whose name was Abraham, who lived with his old mother, he only had few coins and a cat.

One day he went to the city and noticed a chest. He wanted to buy it, so he took all his money and purchased the chest.

The mother got very angry on seeing the chest, now they had no money.

Abraham tried to open the chest but it was locked. When he finally opened it, a big snake came out. But it was not really a snake, it was a girl covered with the snake' skin.

She told him that she had escaped from her kidnappers and she had hided in that chest.

She asked Abraham to take her to her father, and the father would give him a lot of money. The boy accepted. While walking, the girl told him that the father would give him a stone, that if he threw it on the ground, it would give him a beautiful castle with everything that his heart desired. The king was not very happy about the stone, but he give it to the boy anyway.

On the way back Abraham found himself in a big field with no water, no plants and decided to see if the stone would actually work.

He threw the stone down and a beautiful building appeared. He ate, drank and he heard a knock at the door. He opened and there were some poor merchants asking for food.

Abraham gave them water and food, till someone asked him how he had that beautiful castle in the desert.

Abraham told them the whole story. One of the merchant told him he also had a magic ring, and if he rubbed the ring four slaves would come out and do everything he wanted to. The merchant asked for a trade, after a while the boy agreed. But as soon as he had agreed the castle disappeared. He tried rubbing the ring and four strong slaves appeared.

He asked them to find the merchant and take his stone back from him. They left and after few minutes the slaves came back with his stone.

Abraham kept walking and he arrived in another beautiful region and decided to have the castle there. He also rubbed the ring and 4 slaves appeared. One day the king's daughter came by looking for Abraham. She asked for the ring and he gave it to her. But then he was sorry for having given the ring to the girl. His faithful cat helped him, he went in the castle in the princess's bedroom and stole the ring. Few months later the young man asked the princess to marry him. He went to get his mother and they all lived happily thereafter.

CHAPTER 36

THE STORY OF THE ELEPHANT TRUNK

Many years ago, elephants did not have a long nose. In fact they were very different. The face looked like a bear, but with less fur. One day, in the savannah, a little elephant was born. He was very curious and he bothered all the other animals. One day he went to the giraffe and asked, "Why is your neck so long?" She was very touchy, did not know the answer, so she send him away. Then the little elephant discouraged went to the hippopotamus, and asked, "Why are you so fatty." The hippopotamus also got angry and send him away.

The little elephant kept walking around and thought to go and talk to the alligator.

As soon as he saw him and was about to ask him a naughty question, the alligator who was faster, took the little elephant by the nose and shook him. From then on, the elephant's nose was long. That is why is called a trunk.

CHAPTER 37

THE PIGEON AND THE ANT

In a very hot day, the ant had decided to go to the river to drink some fresh water. While drinking she lost her balance and fell in the water. Because of being so small the current took her far away from her ant hill. In the meantime a pigeon was getting some little pieces of grass and wood to make a nest. She saw that the ant was having problems, so she went into the water and picked up the little ant from the river. The ant thanked her for her kindness, and walked away. After one hour a hunter saw the pigeon and was taking aim. Fortunately the ant saw it in time and bit the man's ankle. The hunter, that was about to shoot, started screaming and missed the target. So the little ant had returned the favor to her friend the pigeon.

CHAPTER 38

THE FLOWER AND THE SNAIL

Once upon a time a little flower had been born in a large green pasture. Unfortunately the flower was all by himself, and he was very sad. One day it was very hot and the flower kept thinking. "It would be so nice if there was another flower I could talk to."

Then he heard a noise and looked down. There was a very tiny snail that was looking for shadow.

The little snail looked at the flower and said, "Hello, flower, may I please sit under your petals, so that I have a little shadow."?

The flower did not know what to say. He had never seen a snail and was a little scared, so he did not say anything. The little snail, saw his hesitation and said, "Don't worry, I will not hurt you, and I will keep you company by telling you stories."

The flower accepted and from then on the snail would go to him and tell him stories. The flower was so happy to finally have someone to talk to.

Summer came and the little flower was getting very sick, and asked the snail why. She told him that every flower at a certain point must travel, his pollen would be taken by the wind and will go in another field, and then after a while little flowers will be born. At this news, the flower became very sad, and started crying, and told the snail, that he did not want to go away from her, because he really cared for her. The little snail promised that she will be there when it would take place, and she will make sure that the pollen will fall in a beautiful place and that she will be there.

And so it happened. When you walk and see a little snail in the shadow of a flower, you can approach and listen to the beautiful stories that she says.

CHAPTER 39

THE VAIN CROW

A crow was very tired of her plumage. She wanted something beautiful that everyone will envy.

She constantly complained with the other crows, she wanted to wear something colored so that everyone would admire her. One day she found on the ground some plume from a peacock. She picked them up and put them on herself. She met some other friends, and walked by. Some laughed, but she did not care because they could not understand how beautiful she was.

So, she lost all her friends, but she did not care, she was finally beautiful. She went between other peacocks, hoping that they would accept her. But they all laughed because she was half crow and half peacock. She was crushed, so she decided to go back to her old friend, but they all asked her to go away and never come back. So the crow remained alone because of her vanity.

CHAPTER 40

THE WOLF AND THE CRANE

One day, the wolf, that was eating away, swallowed a bone that remained in his throat. He had always been violent, but now he was very docile. He was screaming promising all kind of favors if someone would help him. But no one wanted to help, because they knew how mean he was. They were afraid that the wolf would eat them. Finally after many promises he convinced a crane to help him. The crane put her neck all the way down his jaws, and took the bone out.

"So, what are you going to give me, since I helped you", asked the eager crane.

"1 did not expect this from you, "said the wolf. "ls it not enough that I did not snap your neck while you had it in my mouth.? Now you want a present.? You are really ungrateful."

All the animals knew that the wolf had not changed, he was still surly and ungrateful.

CHAPTER 41

QUE UP—NO SHOWING
BY
DAVID WOMACK WILLS

Sometimes I feel that everyone on earth
Is simply standing in a line.
We take our place at our moment of birth
And spend our allotted time.

No one knows who's in front or behind
As we stand in this endless file
And to the grouping order we are all so blind
But we're living all the while.

We learn in school to graduate
And socialize then take a mate
As life rushes by in a flood of time
We are washed on forward
the head of the line

Then suddenly you arrive at your place in the fore
You struggle and gasp-and then are no more-
But eternally behind you, surging on
Come those hastening to oblivion.

CHAPTER 42

SUSPICION
By
DAVID WOMACK WILLS

Suspicion slithers, stomach on ground,
Slides along silently,
And inserts himself in your life-space,
Switching vowels to sibilant sounds,
For love and trust and honor
Go out as he comes in,
Stuffing the space so silently, ssssh,
Serpent of suspicious soul . . . .

CHAPTER 43

TRANQUIL
BY
DAVID WOMACK WILLS

I know a place at the bottom of a hill,
It's quiet and peaceful with everything still,
Underneath a tree by a flowering vine
A wonderful place for passing time.
You can remember friends of long ago
Your wife and children, a grandchild or so.
And reminiscence the live long day
Bringing back people who passed away.
The older you get, the more are gone
And you begin to feel so all alone.
You are frequently stiff and suffer ills
Couldn't get along without the pills,
In the solitude you restfully find
Your minds floats you backwards to another time
Good wishes all your old friends send
And the heartaches and pain magically end.
You remember all the good times you've had
And you know being old is not so bad.

UP THE CLOCK, DOC
By
David Womack Wills

Many years ago, I was younger I know,
I used to work in a bar.
Our service was fine, the real luxury kind,
And our customers came from afar.

We were on top of an exclusive shop
Which was in turn in a big hotel,
We served to the guests, and all the rest,
And some professionals trade as well.

Our clientele would range from normal to strange,
Gave us particular requests each day,
This was fine there I know, for they had the dough
And boy, did we make them pay.

We had one snob who'd eat com on the cob
Each night while he drank his beer
And would you believe, a cute girl named Eve,
Who wore a kumquat stuck in her ear?

The point of this tale, I'm going to unveil,
It's about a dentist we had
He had such a skill, ran a very smooth drill
But his drinking habits were sad.

Every day at five, he became alive
Burst in with his friends a few
A daiquiri his drink, he'd drink in a wink
In each glass a fresh cashew.

This might seem odd, but the doctor was MOD
And spent money in amounts untold.
We catered to him and his peculiar whim,
Kept cashews on hand by the bowl.

What I'm trying to say, on a most busy day
I noticed it was half-past four.
I filled the blender with ice, daiquiried it twice,
And added a dash of rum more.

The Doc he came in with a beautiful friend,
Our signal "Big Impression" waved
I whipped out his drink, of no problem did think
And reached for one cashew I'd saved.

I picked up the nut, reached for the glass, but
It wasn't a cashew in my hand
The Doctor's girl beamed, the end of the world
seemed,
And I hoped Doc would understand

The nut was hickory, I decided on trickery,
I smoothly put it in the glass
Poured liquor on top, I barely did stop,
And gained confidence that all it would pass.

No time did he waste, his drink he did taste
And then threw up into his hat.
His ears did turn blue, then his face it did too,
And he chocked, "My God, what is that?"

I had to confess, I had done my best,
For I was rushed so by the clock
"That's a special drink, very good, I think,
For it's a hickory daiquiri, Doc'!"

CHAPTER 45

A CAT NAMED FIFI

There was a cat whose name was Fifi, and he was quite famous for killing mice. One day he went to the country side hunting for sparrows. The mice met in the cellar. "We need to find a remedy," said the oldest mouse.

"We need to cut his long nails, take his teeth, so he cannot kill any more mice."

Not everyone agreed. Another old mouse said, "I have seen a dog that belongs to the lady upstairs, that wears a bell, and that bell rings every time he moves." So the old mouse pulled out from a bag a collar with a bell, that he had taken from the dog's bed.

"Let us put this collar and the bell on the cat, so we can hear him when he comes closer."

They all applauded, they were promising extra cheese for him, but a little mouse asked. "And who is going to place that collar on the cat?"

No one was brave enough, so they left confused and no decision was made.

CHAPTER 46

YOUR 55 1/2 YEAR BIRTHDAY
By
DAVID WOMACK WILLS

Your half birthday is the answer,
To my being cured from prostate cancer.
So every birthday counts as two,
'Cause I'll be here much longer with you.
Enjoy our time and always laugh,
And celebrate on birthdays and the half.
While we age just half as much,
And we get younger with every touch.
Remember give thanks to heaven above,
For all our years and for all our love

As Always
Dave

CHAPTER 47

THE SLY TURTLE

One day a very hungry fox saw a frog on the river of a lake and decided to eat it. But the turtle knew what the fox was about to do, so she bit the fox's tail. The fox got very angry and decided to eat the turtle, but his teeth started hurting, he was not even able to scratch the shell. So the fox said to the turtle, "I am throwing you in the fire."

"Thanks," said the turtle, "I was getting cold, so I can get warmer."

The fox changed his mind, "I will throw you in the air, so when you fall you will die."

"Thanks," answered the turtle, "So now I can finally play with the clouds."

"Okay, then I will throw you in the water."

"NO," screamed the turtle. "I do not know how to swim, please don't kill me this way."

The fox threw her into the lake, but the turtle knew how to swim, so she sneered and went to her friend, the frog. Together they started laughing at the fox, who did not know how to swim, so he could not do anything about it.

CHAPTER 48

THE LEGEND OF THE CORALS

Long time ago, a fisherman was coming back home with his boat. The sky was very dark, not just because it was getting late, but clouds were forming at the horizon. At a certain point he heard a scream. He knew was a girl, she was sad and scared, her cry was as loud as a thunder. He was not very brave but decided to help the girl. He stopped his boat by the rocks, and tried to carry it on the dirt. The fisherman was so much in a hurry that did not realize that his fish were about to fall. In fact a fish fell on a branch that was floating in the water. The girl kept yelling and screaming because a bad fairy, jealous of her beauty, had tied her to a rock next to the river. The sea was cold and the waves high. The fisherman jumped in the sea, to free the young girl from the chains. In the meantime the little branch of the tree was becoming red because of the fishes' blood. And because it was quite cold, it was hardening. The Sea Queen Mary took the branch and placed it around her neck. Then when she got tired of it, she threw it in the water, and that is how the coral was born.

CHAPTER 49

THE WIZARD'S DAUGHTER

The wizard had a daughter to marry. The girl was beautiful but sad, because her father would never had boys come and see her, but instead he made them disappear. In the village, a young man Alessio wanted to see her anyway. On the way, he met an old man that give him this advice. "The way to the castle is full of traps. Don't fall in. When you get there go next to her, and follow her step by step."

Alessio did what he had been told, and arrived to the castle. The wizard complimented him, on how smart he had been.

"Tomorrow there is another challenge."

The next day he found in front of the castle a very wild horse. Alessio knew that that horse was the wizard. He knew it because his daughter had told him so the night before. She had told him in order to tame the horse, he needed to hit him on the head three times.

The young man, did what she had told him and was ready for the third challenge.

"Tomorrow, you must recognize my hand between hundred of them. But it is going to be easy, because on my little finger I have a scar." Alessio was able to recognize her hand. So the wizard had no choice but have them get married. And the day they got married they were so happy that even the wizard celebrate it with happiness.

CHAPTER 50

WHY THE SUN IS IN THE SKY

The sea had always been on the land, and where they were valleys. The sun did not always lived in the sky. Many years ago the sun was on top of a mountain. The sun and the sea were very good friends. Many times the sun will come down from the mountain and went to visit the sea, and the two will spend time playing. The sun always asked to the sea why he was not coming on top of the mountain, but the sea could not go. After a while the sun was getting offended in the way the sea was behaving, so he got angry and asked, "Why are you not coming to my house on top of the mountain. I am a good person, my house is big and I have plenty food to give you."

The sea said, "My dear friend, I am big and deep. You are my friend, and I don't want to hurt your feelings."

The sun kept insisting and the sea finally decided to climb on the mountain. He was so huge, that he submerged the mountain, but the sun was proud and did not want to admit that he had been wrong.

So the sea kept on rising and soon he had covered all the mountains. The sun, worried of being killed, went up in the sky. The sea returned back home, but the sun remained in the sky instead of the top of the mountain.

CHAPTER 51

PEANUT

There were two married people, they lived in the country and cultivate their own land. But they were sad because they did not have any children. But one day, a baby was born. He was so small that could fit in the palm of a hand. Mom and dad called him Peanut. Everyone will say: "Don't worry he will grow." But the baby remained small. The father was a little bit disillusioned.

"How can he work in the fields," he thought. "He cannot even reach the cows."

One night the boy while asleep, heard some very strange noises. He got up from his small bed and went to see what was going on. They were thieves in the house and stealing chickens. The little boy, hiding behind the door, started screaming, "What are you doing, stop stealing these chickens."

The thieves could not seen him, so they got scared, they thought that there was a ghost, so they ran away without taking the chickens.

Nights later they decided to come back to steal the ox. Peanut, awaken by a small noise, went to the stable and was hiding in the ox's ear.

"Please don't take me", he started screaming.

The thieves thought that the ox could talk, and they ran away promising never to return to that hunted house.

The father had heard all of this, and told Peanut," You are a wonderful boy." And from then on, he was very proud of his son.

CHAPTER 52

THE SUN IN LOVE

Once upon the time the Sun fell in love with a little star. He saw her every morning in the sky talking with other planets and other stars. She would flirt, she will look herself in the comets and she was always the first one to catch the first ray of the sun so she could shine more than the other stars. The Sun, had completely fallen in love with her, and decided to give her a present. He extended his ray, took a white garland from the cloud and made a rose and give it to the star. The star laughed and the Sun was really ashamed and hurt, he became all red and threw himself in the sea so no one could see how embarrassed he was.

The next day the Sun came up again and decided to give her another present. This time with his long ray stole the tail of the comet and gave it to the star. Again the star started laughing, so the Sun, was so offended that he hided behind a mountain.

The third day he was quite upset of the beautiful star behavior, so he decided to disappear, and went around sad, and hiding behind the planets.

All of the sudden a beautiful comet appeared, went next to him and said, "My dear Sun, if you continue to hide you will have all of us die from the cold. We need you and your warmth. Please do not abandon us."

The Sun was so taken from these words that he came out and start giving warmth to all the comets.

CHAPTER 53

AN ENDLESS STORY

Once upon a time there was a king that wanted for his daughter to get married, but only to a man that could tell him a story without an end. If he did not succeed he had to leave the reign.

A long line formed in front of the gate of the castle. Many princes arrived from all over the world, they tried to tell a story, but all had an ending. They did not know how to say a story without an end.

One day a farmer stopped by the castle wondering if he could succeed.

The king started listening to his story.

"A man decided to built a huge granary that would reach the sky, and as big as all the fields put together. At the top he left a hole so small that only one ant at the time could go thru it. The first ant went in and brought a little grain of corn, then the second, then the third . . . ."

The story had no end, since to fill in the all granary would have taken forever. The king got tired so he gave his daughter in marriage to the smart farmer.

CHAPTER 54

WHY WE HAVE DESERTS

Many centuries ago, at the beginning of time, the land was rich of fields, gardens, forests. The dirt had been created, and it was so rich that fruits and trees were in abundance. In the village, at the border of the forest lived two men. Each one of them had a huge field and they were quite wealthy.

Then dryness began, the two men met and tried to figure out a way to beat the dry weather. Time went by, and the land had no water and was very dry, nothing would grow. The trees started dying, so the grasses. Mark, one of the man, decided to go to God and ask him for rain. He walked, walked, and finally was able to meet him. God told him that he had assigned to some men many easy jobs. One man was taking care of the wind, that will blow, another one to be sure that the sun would come out, and another man to remember to make rain.

"Maybe the man has forgotten about the rain. Go to him and remind him of his duty," said God.

Mark started his voyage, arrived at the person's house, and called him, but he was not there, so he thought maybe he was dead.

"What am I to do now.?"

God from then on decided that he will take care of the wind, rain, sun, but the zone where rain had not been for a while became a desert.

CHAPTER 55

THE BABY STOLEN BY THE FAIRIES

A beautiful spring morning a little girl went out to get flowers to give to her mom and dad. While she was walking along the river, she heard laughs. She followed the sound and it was coming from the hills. The sound was coming from a cave. The little girl approached the cave and she saw fairies dancing and singing. She was astonished and scared and she ran away, and told everything to her parents. The parents were terrified, they knew that the fairies would come during the night and take the little girl away because she had seen them. The parents did not say anything to the little girl not to scare her. The parents went to see an old lady and she told them "The fairies only have one chance to steal the little girl. If they cannot take her the first time, they cannot do it again. So be sure that you keep the little girl in your house, no noise for the whole night."

Mom and dad went home, locked all doors and windows and made sure that the floor and the steps would not make any noise, and be sure that the little girl would be asleep. They took all the clocks from the wall, then they sat in the living room and waiting for the night to finish. When the fairies arrived, the house was completely quiet. They were about to leave when a little dog started barking, mom and dad ran to the little girl room. The bed was empty, and they knew they will never see her again.

CHAPTER 56

THE MAN FISH

In a far land, at the river, lived a young girl that had refused many suitors. One day a man knocked at the door, and this man was fascinating. They talked for a while and the woman fell in love with him,

She said, "I like for you to meet my parents."

"I am very poor, it is better if I do not meet them, they are not going to like me."

The two lovers spend all day together. The man was in reality the spirit of the river, and his job was to take care of the sea and fishes. In the village it lacked water to wash, and to drink and to give it to the animals and it lacked fishes.

The woman said to the villagers, "It is your fault, if I did not have to hide from all of you, and could be with him, we could take care of the river."

The villagers got together and decided to accept their strange marriage. The woman disappeared for three days, in the meantime it started to rain, the river was full again, and there was water and fishes again.

Then the woman returned, and told them that she now lived under the river, and there was water everywhere. After few months she came back to introduce her baby to her family and then she disappeared forever.

CHAPTER 57

THE MAGIC ROAST

In a winter evening a man and his wife were talking of their neighbor, much richer then them.

"If I could have anything I wished, I would be happier than they are." said the woman.

At that moment a fairy appeared. "Ask three wishes, only three, and I'll fulfill them."

"I would like to be beautiful, rich and refined," said the wife.

"I would like to be in good health, happy and have a long life," said the husband.

"Why have a long life, if you are poor," said the wife.

"Let us think till tomorrow what we want, and we will ask for it," said the husband.

"Okay," said the wife.

"With this beautiful fire I would like a piece of roast for our supper," said the man without thinking.

From the chimney fell a big piece of meat.

"Now, because of you we only have two wishes left," said the wife.

"I am so angry that I would like for a wart to grow on your nose."

And so it happened.

"I will ask to be rich so you can get well," said the man.

"Are you crazy? I want for the wart to fall off right now," said the woman.

The wart fell and the woman said to the husband. "The fairy has taught us a good lesson. It is better to have less wishes, and live as well as we can."

And that evening they ate the roast smiling away.

CHAPTER 58

THE LEGEND OF THE POISON IVY

It was a beautiful summer day. Milly and Sally were laying under the sun. Milly, she was six years old, was laying on the grass. "Why poison Ivy hurts." she asked the bigger sister, 8 years old. The sister had no idea.

"Let's ask dad."

The dad was planting potatoes.

"Hello, children, what are you doing?"

"Nothing special," said Sally," we would like to know why poison Ivy hurts."

"I am not sure," said the dad, "but they told me a story about it. Do you want to hear it?"

The two little girls screamed of joy, "Yes, Yes, we want to hear the story."

"Long time ago in a field there was a little plant of poison Ivy. She was so sad because no one liked her. She was avoided by everyone because she would irritate their skins, but she could not do anything about it. One day a beautiful butterfly landed on her leaves. The poison Ivy asked why she was not afraid.

"You are perfect to look after my eggs during the winter," said the butterfly.

"Of course, I will be honored," said the poison ivy.

So the butterfly left her precious eggs. The poison ivy protected them from snow, wind, hail. No animals could touch the eggs.

In the springtime, from the eggs came out the caterpillars that became butterfly. When summer came beautiful butterflies were flying around the poison ivy.

"Thank you, said the butterfly mother. You are the strongest and the safest." And from then on, every winter, the poison ivy protects the eggs of the butterflies."

CHAPTER 59

WHY THE CHICKEN SCRATCHES THE EARTH

Many years go, the chicken and hawk were great friends. One day the chicken went to visit the hawk, who was playing with a colored stone.

The chicken said, "What a beautiful rock, my children would love it."

"Take it with you and let your children play with it," said the hawk, "but be careful not to loose it, because I really like it and want it back."

The chicken took the stone to her house. The baby chicks played for hours. Since they did not know about the agreement with the hawk, they hided the stone in a hole.

"So, only us can find it again."

But unfortunately they forgot where they had hidden the stone. When the hawk came to visit the chicken to take the stone back, the chicken said, "Of course, let me ask my chicks."

But no one knew where it was. The chicken started scratching the earth, the hawk was becoming more and more nervous. He waited for a long time, then he became angry.

"Because your baby chicks lost it, I will be back every day till you will find my stone,"
and the hawk took one the baby chicks with him.

From then on, the hawk comes back to take one baby chick at the time, and the chicken scratches the earth hoping to find the colored stone.

CHAPTER 60

THE GIRL OF THE MELON

Once lived an old couple without children. One day the wife went to the river to wash her clothes and saw a beautiful melon floating in the river. She decided to grab it and take it home to share with her husband. When they opened the melon, inside there was a small baby. They were so happy, they had wanted children for a long time.

Time went by and the little girl became a beautiful young lady.

Everyone loved her because she was so gentle and generous. She had become engaged to a young man. In the forests lived a bear, very jealous of this girl. One day, while her parents were away and the girl was alone in the house, the bear came at her door. The girl opened the door and the bear took the girl, locked her in a cave and took her form.

But the parents knew something was not right, she was not pleasant, she was rude, and she did not feed her cat, and talked bad about her fiancée. The cat, who was very smart, knew what had happened, so he left and went into the forest. The girl in the meantime had become friend with the dwarfs of the forests. The cat asked the dwarfs where she was, they showed him the cave, and the cat was able to free her.

The bear left chased by the animals, and never came back again

CHAPTER 61

VALENTINE DAY—2007
BY
DAVID WOMACK WILLS

I can't believe it happened so fast,
Another year has raced on past.
I wasn't watching; didn't seen it go,
But I enjoyed your company, even so,

It's nice to spend my time with you,
We have so many thing to do.
Time with you is never wasted,
And you have the sweetest kisses I've tasted!

We fit together like a lock and key,
With me for you and you for me.
I get upset that you work so hard,
Both on the house and in the yard.

I realize I'm lucky to have you here,
To hold and keep as a thing so dear.
I wish I could make you rest a bit,
And do more puzzles as you sit.

I hope next year is as good as the last,
And won't rush by, so dog gone fast.
I'd like to rest and keep you mine,
And hold the hand of my Valentine

Love ya—Dave

CHAPTER 62

CHRISTMAS IN THE AIR FORCE
BY
DAVID WOMACK WILLS

T'was the night before Christmas and all through the base,
Most everyone off duty but the guards were in place
The stars were shining, it was a beautiful night,
The sentry dogs walking, and security up tight.
Then the tower operator was startled to hear,
"Request clearance to land, me and nine little reindeer."
"Tower to reindeer, go round for a while,
For your transmission to us are not the approved style".
"HO .... HO .... HO ...! The voice came back,
"you guys down there, are on the wrong track."
"Quick, George, call Ops." The tower did say,
"That place with one light is landing the wrong way.
For that is all wrong as the regulation shows
With one red running light on the tip of the nose."
The Flight Safety Board did quickly convene,
But could not do much with such a flying machine.
The little fat pilot wore a fur-trimmed red suit,
With a hat that matched it, and a black leather jump boot.
The Security Police did all they could do,
They called Helping Hand, and a Covered Wagon too.
While the little fat man, away did he dash,
Finished his business and returned in a flash.
His packages everywhere on base he did scatter
Because his big sack was noticeably flatter.
One leap to the sleigh, with his finger on his nose,
The sleigh and the reindeer into the air they all rose.
They went down the runway and passed out of sight,
Shouting, "Merry Christmas to All, and To All a Good Night."

CHAPTER 63

SOIXANTE

BY

DAVID WOMACK WILLS

The time has come again to say
Lots of love on your birthday.
The years they seem to ship on past
I can't keep this year away from last.

At least my love remains so true
And I can not love anyone but you.
I am sure that it will come to pass
My love for you will last and last.

The world goes on at a frantic pace
Still we have no time to waste.
There are many things that are still to do
And I will only complete a few.

We'll complete these things hand-in-hand
Because you're lady, and I'm your man.
Thank you for all the love and care
You can take me most anywhere.

It breaks my heart when you're burdened down
Your classroom stuffed with children abound.
It'll get better in the by-and-by
But still it makes me want to cry.

We've had some bad days, but now they're good
We get along just fine we should.
With a heart-felt prayer from heavens above
You're birthday present is a world of love

CHAPTER 64

VALENTINE DAY 2001
36 YEARS
By
DAVID WOMACK WILLS

Valentine's Day is here again
Pushing through the turmoil and din
Of working, loving and everyday life
That I luckily spend with my darling wife.

Time for us goes racing by
Passing as quickly as clouds in the sky.
Weeks are days and months tumble behind
We're getting older we suddenly find.

But aging together is not so bad
After the thirty-six years we've already had
Going together and hand in hand
Another thirty six I sure could stand.

The cracks in the family that you feel
Are breaks in the heart and need to heal
We don't know why they come about
But maybe time will smooth them out.

If I should go before you are ready,
Truly your life should still stay steady
If you remember, I can never die,
You'll see me at the corner of your eye.

There is too much of me all around
Things I've done everywhere bound
I'll always be inside of you
And in everything you try to do.

Maybe someday you will meet a friend
Who can stay with you until the end
Which probably is not the end at all
But just the time you get your call.

I'll be here and love you true
For we still have much more to do
I loved you then, I love you still
With the help of God, I always will

37 YEARS ANNIVERSARY
BY
DAVID WOMACK WILLS

I don't know what I would do
If as old as I am, I didn't have you
I stumble around, and throw things down,
My shirts everywhere and my socks around

Most of the time I'm in your hair
Even though I'm in a chair
And still you don't get mad at me
When I look at you, it's a smile I see.

All these years, what we've have been through
With Spang and Bitburg, and Shaw travels too,
I've gotten mad and fussed at you
And we both knew it wasn't true.

When I've been drinking and come home late,
You've treated me like we were in a date
Then smiled at me and held my head
Gave me a kiss, and send me to bed.

When I got out and started to teach
When I had problems to you I'ld reach
You helped solve just any wrong
And turned your lovely smile back on.

Problems with the kids, and money too,
Your beautiful smile just pulled us through
You've fulfilled my needs for all these years
With heartache, deaths, and many tears.

Let's start counting again in our little heaven
And try for another thirty seven
If we don't get to reach this, I have to say
I'll love you more on every day

Happy Anniversary cara

CHAPTER 66

39 YEARS WOW!
By
DAVID WOMACK WILLS

We've been living together as man and wife
More than many people's entire life
No matter what our old friends said
We worked very hard and came out ahead.
The secret of this thing you see,
Is I love you and you love me.

There is never you or me, to cause a fuss
We talk it over, and then there's only us.
If there's a problem that stumps just one,
Then double on it and get it done.
The kids, and work, and where we go
Money or healthy or floating, you know

Sort it out and put 'em in line.
We handle each one, and every time.
Then we hold hands and kiss good night
And everything just comes out right.
The house is fine, the lawns' so neat
When the weeds are gone we've got it beat.

What I'm trying to say, my love so true
I'm glad I gave my life to you.
Another ten years I'ld like to see
With me for you and you for me.

Happy Anniversary, Cara

CHAPTER 67

VALENTINE 2003
AND ALL THOSE YEARS
By
David Womack Wills

The second month is the time
Most guys are looking for a Valentine
I used to have to do this too
Until I made an acquaintance with you.

I begged, pleaded and even whined
Until you agreed to be my Valentine.
And all these years I've had a hold on you
By staying nice and sweet and always true.

Thirty-eight years we've been a pair
No matter when fortune took us where
I had to convince you that I'm your man
By kissing your cheek and holding your hand.

You always responded with love in kind
With lips as sweet as a glass of wine
I've forever said to all around
You have the prettiest pair of lips in town,

And all these years that have flowing away
Were the greatest of all, I have to say.
And we faced them all hand in hand
And together we learned to understand.

I don't need to ask if you'll be mine
For all these years, you 'were my Valentine.
And when we go to Heavens above
We'll be carried there on the wings of love

Love Always Dave

CHAPTER 68

MERRY CHRISTMAS 2004
By
David Womack Wills

I don't really know where all the time goes,
Because I spend it all here with Rose.
That sends my feelings up to the sky
And then I don't see the time zoom by.

She happily fulfills my very need
And keeps me very happy indeed.
She's a pretty lady with a smile so nice
I want to kiss her once or twice.

Time rolls on, week after week
I grow older and I'm becoming weak
You are much younger and full of pep
And all of your beauty you have kept.

One thing different you did this year
You said, "No gift exchange for us, my dear."
I gave you just token things, you see.
While you piled luxury gifts on me.

I'm not angry and don't hold a grudge,
Even if on gifts you did fudge.
I'll make up next Christmas time
And all your gifts will be of the costly kind

Merry Christmas, Honey

CHAPTER 69

MOTHER'S DAY—2005
By
David Womack Wills

I'm always surprised when it's Mother Day
And another year has slipped away
Then we all go out to EPCOT see
And there get our picture made for free

We past them all on the freezer door.
Where's room on there for many more
When I look at them, I can each time see
How very well you take care of me.

Without you here I wouldn't stick around
And nowhere else could I be found
There'd be no sense in my existing on
If I had to do it all alone.

Life without you my love is no life at all
Without someone who cares and always on call.
After all these years, I wouldn't want to try
And watch the empty years go limping by

So you keep on living and I'll try too
Until you retire at eighty-two
I will be just ninety-five
And no one will be sure I am also alive.

CHAPTER 70

ANOTHER BIRTHDAY
By
DAVID WOMACK WILLS

After watching you and staying near
And seeing the birthday you have each year,
To make it joyous you always try
And all a year—I wonder why?

What's wrong with the one you last years had?
It was kind of pretty and not all bad.
It was curved on the front and round on the end.
And a message of maturity it did send.

I think it really would be fine,
If you went back to fifty-nine.
Or twenty-eight, or forty-three,
As long as you stay here, along with me.

We should good-bye to birthdays say,
And eat a cake on your Name Day.
Without any help we get old soon.
It's a good thing we're on our Honeymoon.

I love you now, I'll love you then
And next year we'll start all over again.
I'm staying alive just to be with you,
Even if the years are few.

Your school situation is rough this time.
I hope next year it will be fine.
It hurts me 'cause there's nothing I can do
To make the floating easier on you.

One nice thing Rock Lake seems to do
I get an extra half-hour to spend with you.
That makes me want to sing and shout
'Cause really that's what it's all about.

Happy un-birthday, cara
I love you
Dave